Pig in jeans

NEW HOUSE, SAME UNDERWEAR

SUMMER+MUU™
summerandmuu.com

Paperback:
ISBN-13: 978-1-77447-010-7

Published by Summer and Muu
Printed and Made in United States
Summer and Muu, Summer and Muu Kids and associated logos are trademarks and/or regis-
tered trademarks of Summer and Muu.

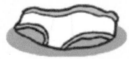

NEW HOUSE, SAME UNDERWEAR

is dedicated to my dearest friend, John.

Although you have
moved into a new home
quite far away,
our friendship will always
stay the same.

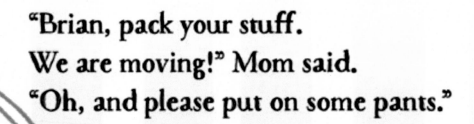

"Brian, pack your stuff.
We are moving!" Mom said.
"Oh, and please put on some pants."

"NOW?! BUT YOU NEVER TOLD ME!"
Brian was in shock.

8

"Well, either way, we are moving," Mom insisted.
"Stop hiding in the toilet and go pack."

"Oh sweetie, why don't you want to move?"
Mom asked.

"I don't want to move because our house is a lot of fun."

"**AND** I don't want to lose my friends," Brian said. "I love playing with them."

"Don't worry, Brian," Mom said. "You won't lose your friends."

"You can keep in touch by drawing pictures and mailing them to your friends."

"They will love receiving your mail!"

"You can talk to them on the phone."

"You guys can also connect through video chats!"

"See, Brian? Even though you're moving to a new house, your friendships will stay the same."

"You know what else stays the same?"

MY UNDERWEAR?

No, silly — the people you love!

"Your house may have changed,
but loved ones will always stay the same."

"Do you know why our house is fun?" Mom started to explain. "It's because **WE** live inside the house."

"It's **FUN** because Dad flips you upside down."

WHEEEE!

"It's FUN because your sister plays hide and seek with you."

"It's **FUN** because Mommy
reads you funny books at night."

"As long as you're living with
the people you love,
it doesn't matter where you move to.
Everywhere will be fun!"

Right away, Brian packed his underwear into boxes.

He packed some into a bag,
and wore one on his head.

Everyone started carrying boxes out of the house.
"Brian, please help load the truck," Mom said.

23

"IT'S GOING TO BE AN AWESOME MOVING DAY,"
Mom said.

When they arrived at their new house,
they were shocked to see nothing in the truck.
OH NO!
They didn't close the back and everything had fallen out!

Just as they were wondering
what to do, Brian's friends showed up,
carrying their boxes and furniture.

Brian was so surprised to see his friends.
He asked, "Guys! How did you find me?"

"We followed your underwear!"
Sloth answered.

"My mom was driving,
and we kept going and
going and going."

"We drove for 10 hours!!"

Brian couldn't wait to show his friends around.

COME ON GUYS! LET ME SHOW YOU MY NEW HOUSE!

WRONG HOUSE

Soon, it was time to say goodbye.

My mom told me that you live quite far, so we can't play with each other like before. But we can still see each other in video chats!

OR TALK ON THE PHONE!

OR MAIL DRAWINGS TO EACH OTHER!

"Are we still best friends forever?" Brian asked.

BEST FRIENDS FOREVER.

PICK A PATH. WHERE ARE YOU MOVING TO?

Hope you enjoyed the book!
Please leave me a ♥
review on Amazon!

FREE COLORING PRINTABLES:
SummerandMuu.com/freebie

Made in the USA
Monee, IL
05 July 2021